A Vacc... MM Mouse

Written by Jill Eggleton
Illustrated by Jennifer Cooper

Pop and Harry put
their bags in the car.
MM Mouse sat
by her cage.
Her whiskers went
wobble, wobble.

"No, MM," said Harry.
"You can't come.
We're staying
in a hotel.
Mice can't stay
at hotels."

Harry gave MM
a bag of chips and
some cheese.
"You won't be hungry,"
he said.

But MM Mouse didn't
want to stay behind.
When Harry wasn't
looking, she sneaked
into his pocket.

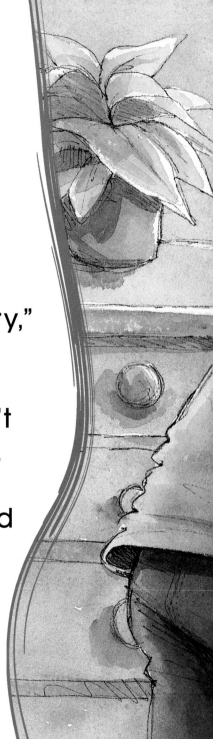

4

Pop and Harry
got to the hotel.
Miss Molly was
behind the desk,
and lots of people
were in line.

"A big room is
two hundred dollars,"
said Miss Molly.
"A small room
is fifty dollars."

"Two hundred
dollars!" said Pop.
"We can't stay in
a big room."

7

MM Mouse's whiskers
went **wobble, wobble**.
She jumped out of
Harry's pocket and
ran over the floor.

"A mouse!"
shouted a woman.
"I saw a mouse."

Miss Molly looked
over the desk.
"This is a very good
hotel," she said.
"It doesn't have
any mice."

MM's whiskers went
wobble, wobble.
She ran over feet
and up legs.

"There **is** a mouse!"
shouted the people
in the line.
"We're not staying here!"
And they all ran
out the door.

Miss Molly looked at
Pop and Harry.
"You didn't run
out the door," she said.
"You can have a big
room for fifty dollars."

Pop and Harry
were very happy.
The room had big beds
and a bathtub like
a swimming pool.
They had
a very good vacation.

And MM Mouse had
a very good vacation, too!

Rules

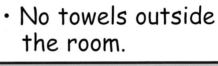

Hotel Rules

- No animals.

- No smoking.

- No towels outside
  the room.

Guide Notes

Title: A Vacation for MM Mouse
Stage: Early (4) – Green

Genre: Fiction
Approach: Guided Reading
Processes: Thinking Critically, Exploring Language, Processing Information
Written and Visual Focus: Rules
Word Count: 253

THINKING CRITICALLY
(sample questions)
- What do you think this story could be about? Look at the title and discuss.
- Look at the cover. Where do you think MM Mouse could go for a vacation?
- Look at pages 2 and 3. Why do you think hotels don't like having mice?
- Look at pages 4 and 5. What do you think MM Mouse will have to do to stay unnoticed by Harry?
- Look at pages 6 and 7. What do you think the big room might have that the little room doesn't have?
- Look at pages 8 and 9. How do you think the people feel when they see a mouse in the hotel?
- Look at pages 10 and 11. Why do you think people don't want to stay in a hotel where there are mice?
- Look at pages 12 and 13. How do you know Pop and Harry are happy to have a big room?

EXPLORING LANGUAGE

Terminology
Title, cover, illustrations, author, illustrator

Vocabulary
Interest words: vacation, hotel, whiskers
High-frequency words: doesn't, behind
Positional words: in, by, into, behind, out, over, up
Compound word: bathtub

Print Conventions
Capital letter for sentence beginnings and names (**MM M**ouse, **P**op, **H**arry, **M**iss **M**olly),
periods, commas, exclamation marks, quotation marks, possessive apostrophes